Not the End of the World

talya baldwin

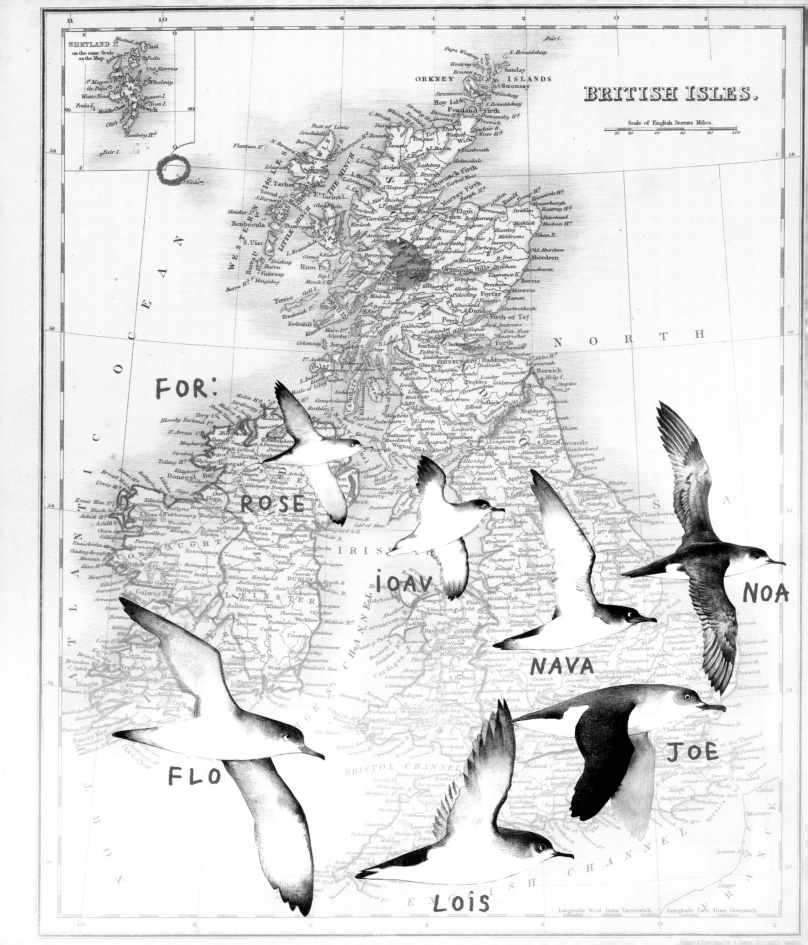

How should a **really** good story begin? Should it start with: 'Once upon a time . . .'? What about: 'Once, in an enchanted land far, far away . . .'?

No, those aren't right, because this is a **true** story about a **real** place.

It's a place hidden behind the waves. The Vikings saw it in their dreams, and sometimes sea birds call its name.

It's a dot on a map. The blink of an eye. The beat of a wing. Storms and songs and stickleback stop by on their travels.

We'll sail there in a birlinn: a beautiful boat from medieval Scotland. It will carry us far out to sea, past the isles of Skye, Harris and Lewis and further still, into the endless blue, battered by wind and salty spray.

This is St Kilda. A tiny group of islands – an archipelago:

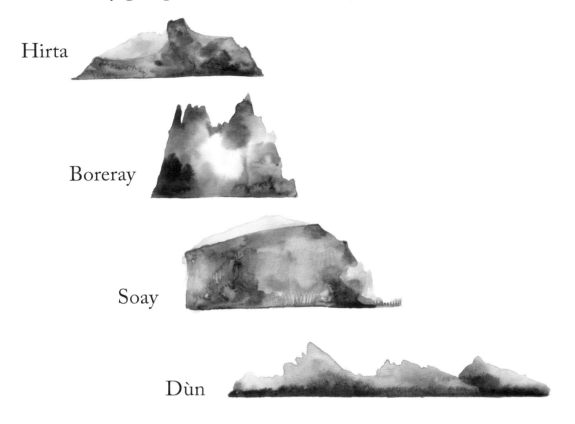

Hirta

Boreray

Soay

Dùn

They call them **The Islands at the End of the World**. But it's **not** the end if you live there, is it? Then the end would be somewhere else entirely:

Hong Kong, maybe.   Or Iceland.   Or Clacton-on-Sea.

There is not a single tree on St Kilda. There are no bees, no roads and no cars. But there are many, many other things!

Look! There are 140 different kinds of beetle.

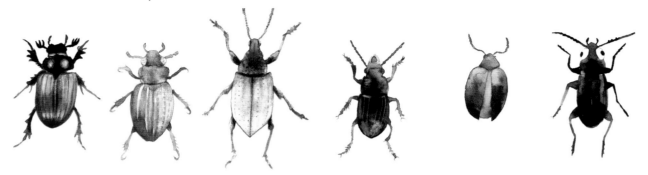

Nearly 100 types of butterfly and moth.

Antler Moth

Dark Arches Moth

Painted Lady

Silvery Moth

Red Admiral

Least Carpet Moth

Atlantic Grey Seal

Buttercup

Bog Pimpernel

Crowberry

St Kilda Field Mouse

There are all sort of flowers, too:

Campion

Common Dog Violet

Insectivorous Sundew

Common Mouse Ear

Angelica

Daisy

Yorkshire Fog

Soay Sheep

White Clover

Scentless Mayweed

Bog Asphodel

But most of all, the air is filled with chattering, with wheelings, rustlings, squabblings and squawks. These are bird islands.

Northern Fulmar

Northern Gannet

Razorbill

Leach's Storm Petrel

Atlantic Puffin

Lesser Black–Backed Gull

Arctic Skua

Northern Mew Gull

Manx Shearwater

Common Guillemot

European Storm Petrel

Greater Black-Backed Gull

Herring Gull

For a very long time, people lived on St Kilda, too.

Here are just a few of them. They were
extraordinary climbers, brave bird hunters.

They spoke Gaelic. They knitted beautiful clothes.

If they needed to, they could survive for months on scrawny gannets and ice-rimmed puddles.

They prayed very hard and danced even harder.

Sometimes, rarely, there were visitors. They brought with them an inkling of another sort of life: of chimneys and chamber pots, of parks and pigeons, of pork pies and the 7.42 to Clapham Junction.

'Goodness!' the visitors would say. 'Where are these people's shoes?'
'No roast beef and Yorkshire pudding?'
'We must teach them to do things properly.'

Then away they would sail, back to the clatter of their trams and tea trays, and St Kilda, such a tiny dot, would seem a made-up place again.

But, of course, behind the waves, where the skuas keep watch and the seals' songs echo in their caves, everything was just as real as ever.

Sometimes, the sea brought gifts.

Other times, it took things away.

But who could you tell, with no phones and no post?

You could shout from the clifftops, but only the puffins would hear.

Or maybe, you could put a message in an old tin and throw it to the waves: 'We've run out of flour!' it might say.

Or: 'We've all caught a cold.'

Or: 'Could you post this to my cousin in Australia?'

Or even: 'Please send help quickly.'

It would be a bit like throwing pennies into a wishing well.

You might get your wish, or . . . you might not.

On St Kilda, people come and go, carried like driftwood on the tide. In a way, maybe everyone who lives here is just passing through.

Here's a First World War sailor, visiting Hirta. He's come to keep watch for enemy submarines and he's building a radio station, too. He'll teach you Morse Code to save you from shouting to the winds. He'll tell you stories of a better life across the sea. But soon, the sea will take him home again.

This is Rachel MacCrimmon.

Rachel MacCrimmon is as old as Hirta itself; pitted and gnarled as a lost sea anchor: smoke-blackened, wind battered. Maybe barnacles cling to her ankles. Maybe she's cooking up a seaweed spell.

She'll give you a sooty
bit of scone; her hens
scratching in the hearth
dust. She'll tell you she'll
never give up this house,
among the last of its
kind.

The smoke stings your
eyes and the mice scuttle
in the darkness. Outside
the storm howls, flinging
its icy might at the walls,
and here you are, warm
as a guga in a feathered
nest. Safe. Loved.

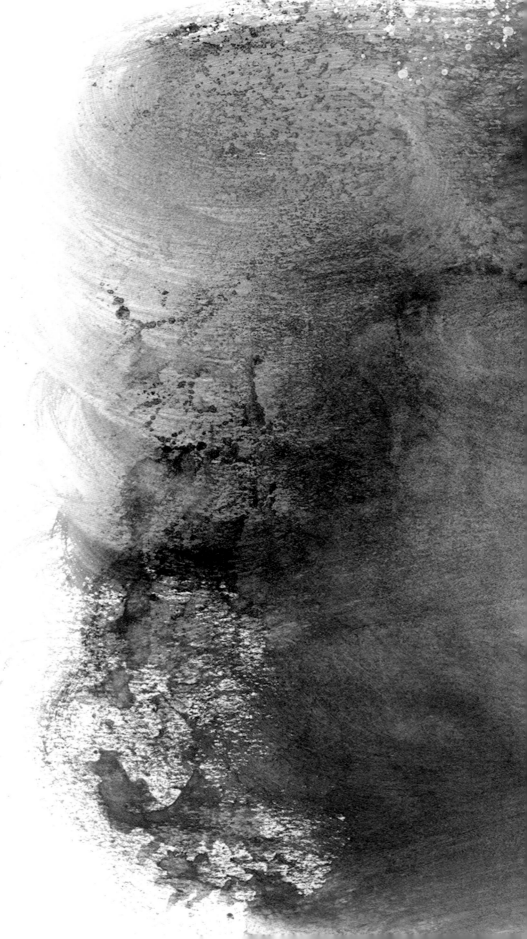

But where are the St Kildans **now**? They listened to the sailors' tales. They wondered and wondered about the wide, wide world.

And in the end, in the blink of an eye, the beat of a wing, they went, too. Maybe they wanted someone to answer when they called.

The people with the parks and pigeons and pork pies, of course, said all sorts of things:

'They were uncivilised.'

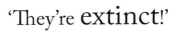

'They're **extinct**!'

'Like the great auk!'

'They just didn't
have what it took
to survive.'

'This is what comes of
walking around with no
shoes on.'

'They got things
all wrong.'

What do **you** think?

I know what I think. The St Kildans aren't
extinct at all – they just went somewhere else.
Their grandchildren are still out there in the
wide, wide world.

Everyone who lives here is just passing through.

So, is this a sad story? Do the puffins look
back as they leave Hirta in a great cloud,
heading for the fishing grounds far, far away?

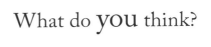

Maybe. But they go, anyway. They're brave, and a little bit excited, and they can feel adventure ruffling their feathers. They know they can't stay for ever. And they know it isn't the end of the world.

You might think St Kilda is a lonely place now, but it's still full of stories if you know where to look! Visitors from all over the world come to find them.

There's the tale of the Amazon, a warrior giantess. Legend says she once hunted here with her greyhounds. Maybe she still does, when no one is watching . . .

There's a snowy owl who sometimes stops by. Who knows what stories he could tell?

Then, there's Lady Grange, banished to Hirta by her grumpy husband in 1732.

And, if you visit, look out for the Blue Men of the Minch on the way. They're watery folk who lurk in the waves. They'll sing you a bit of a sea shanty, and if you don't know the rest, they'll tip up your boat!

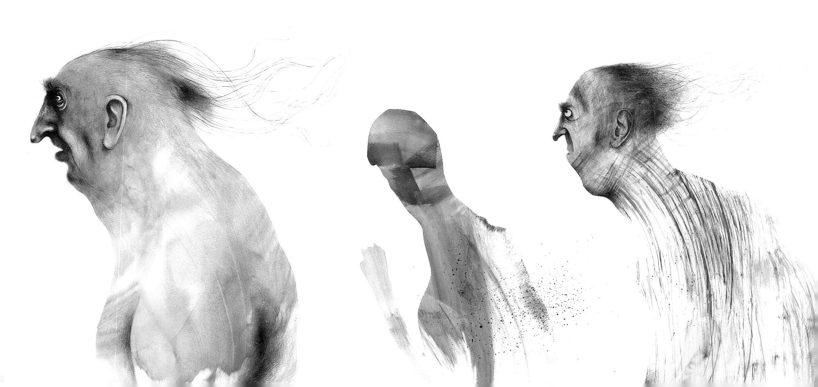

It's a dot on a map. The blink of an eye. The beat of a wing.
But it's **not** the End of the World.

First published in 2024 by BC Books, an imprint of
Birlinn Ltd | West Newington House | 10 Newington Road | Edinburgh EH9 1QS

www.bcbooksforkids.co.uk

ISBN 978 1 78027 888 9

British Library Cataloguing-in-Publication Data
A catalogue record for this book is available on
request from the British Library.

Typeset in Adobe Caslon Pro by The Foundry, Edinburgh
Printed and bound in Latvia by PNB